AF437369

J. L. Huggs

jlhuggs2017@gmail.com

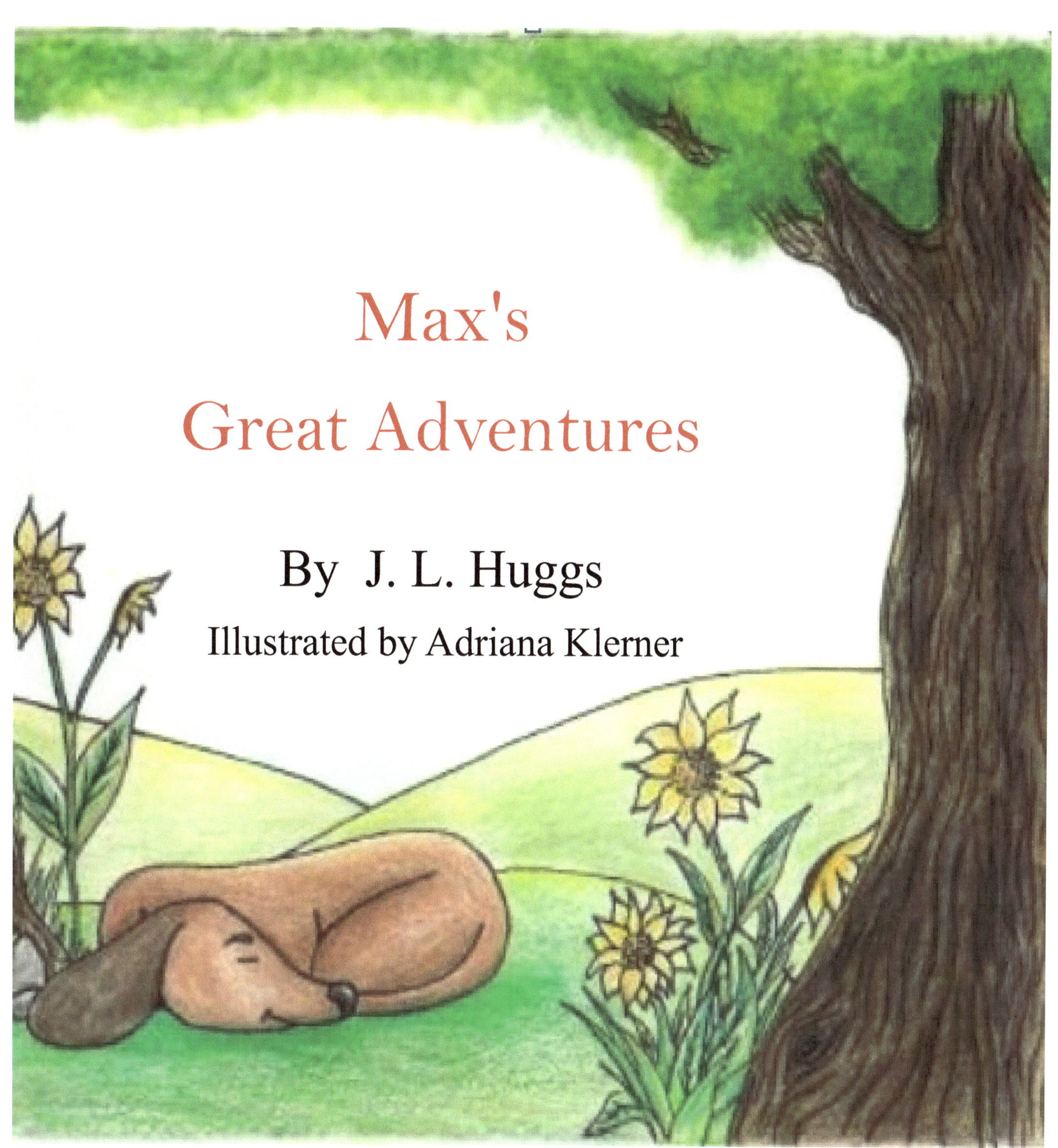

Max's
Great Adventures

By J. L. Huggs

Illustrated by Adriana Klerner

To Luke and Kristen, whose hearts for children gave direction to my purpose.

ZZ

THE ADVENTURE BEGINS

Max spent most of his time playing around the apartment, waiting for his family to come home. Max's family lived in the city. It was filled with tall buildings, restaurants, and busy streets. Max looked forward to his family taking him for a walk each day so he could run in the park – even if he did have to stay on a leash.

Max kept himself very busy each day.   He spent time chewing on his favorite things and playing with his toys. Sometimes he would play chase with himself. Oops! That was not always a good idea. .Most of the time though, Max looked out the window and dreamed of all the things he'd like to do.

Living Room

One day, Max's family started putting all their things into boxes. He knew what this meant; they had done it many times before. Max knew that soon he would go to a new apartment, with new tall buildings, new restaurants, and new busy streets. There would be a new park to run in, and new people to get to know. Max looked forward to the adventure.

On moving day, Max waited patiently while his family loaded their belongings into the moving truck. Finally, he heard the sound of the door being pulled closed. He was so excited! As they drove away, Max watched the family apartment building become smaller and smaller.

As Max watched out the window, he began to notice there were not as many tall buildings. Soon he began to see trees – tall trees, full of deep green leaves. There were big spaces of grass, like his park, but much bigger. Max was so curious. Not only did this drive look different than any of the other family drives he had gone on, but it began to smell   different. He wasn't sure what he smelled, but it was so exciting. Soon, there were so many trees and new smells that Max was aching to get out of the car so he could discover what they were.

Finally, Father said, "We're here!'

They were parked in front of a large, old white house. There was a big porch that wrapped all the way around.

'Could this be there new home? Where were the tall buildings? Where were the   restaurants and busy streets?' he thought.

The car door opened and Max waited for someone to attach his leash. Instead, they called for him to get out and follow them. Max had never been outside without a leash before, but he did as his family asked and got out of the car.

Max was a little unsure, but the urge to run was so strong, that he just couldn't help himself— scents were everywhere! He ran around the house, then back to the car, then back to the front yard again. He ran to the giant tree, where the children were swinging from an old tire that hung from one of the branches. Max smelled something that made his senses go crazy, but he couldn't figure it out. He didn't see anything – he sniffed the ground around the tree; he put his

paws on the tree to sniff higher; he sniffed the air. He searched and searched, but he couldn't

find what it was.

Max followed the scent to the edge of the yard, where he saw a wire fence, tall

grass and a forest of trees in the distance. Max so wanted to continue to follow this

strange new scent, but just as he started under the wire fence, he heard the children call

him to the house. As he walked to the porch, he felt something tugging him toward the

forest of trees. Max turned to look once more before following the children into the

house. He wondered what was beyond the wire fence, tall grass, and forest of trees, and

what was the scent he felt so drawn to follow?

Once inside, Max enjoyed playing chase with the children and exploring the new house. There were large rooms, all filled with boxes, and piles of paper that had been used to wrap things. Max made perfect use of the paper and the boxes, until Mother scolded him and said it was either calm down or outside he'd go. Max voted for outside, but the children begged for him to stay in. They called Max to the laundry room and showed him his bed.

Max was delighted to see his space. He ran and jumped in the middle of his cozy bed, sending his mound of toys flying everywhere. He romped about, turning in circles, getting the cushion just right, then settled down for the night. The children loved on him, rubbed his tummy, and told him goodnight, before going to find Mother and Father.

Max was very tired. It had been a long day, filled with excitement, and he was ready for bed. It didn't take long for him to fall into a deep sleep, and he soon began to dream about his busy day. He could see the tall buildings disappearing into the distance and hear the sounds of his new home.

THUMP!
THUMP! SCRATCH,
SCRATCH, Skreeeeeeech!

Max awoke with a start. He wasn't sure what he heard, but he didn't think he'd dreamed it. Max didn't know what to think. The sound was so strange. He wanted to investigate, but he was stuck in his room. There was a night light glowing from the wall. Mother must have put it there so he could see.

Max climbed out of his bed and sniffed around the room. He found his food and water dish and realized he had been so tired that he hadn't eaten supper before going to sleep. Smelling his food made him realize how hungry he was. Max ate in record time, barely taking time to chew, then went back to his bed. Just as he lay his head down, there it was again – **THUMP!**

Max jumped! He had to find what was making the noise. Moving around the room, Max sniffed every corner, then he came to the door. It was an odd door. Max could feel wind blowing from the edges around the middle. He took a long sniff, pressing his nose to the windy spot. It moved! Max jumped! The door moved! Max again pressed his nose to the windy spot, only this time he pressed harder. It moved more.

Max pushed his head through the opening and saw the porch. He stepped through the door and couldn't believe he was outside! He could come and go outside all on his own! Max stood half inside, half outside feeling the breeze blow his ears. As he stood there, he heard, **THUMP!** He saw a tree branch bumping and scraping against the house as the wind blew it back and forth. Max realized that was nothing to be afraid of.

It was such a nice evening—and the smells! Max could smell so many things! He smelled grass and the yellow flowers from the front of the house; he smelled the bucket of dirt the children had put on the steps;

– and he smelled ----- what did he smell?

There it was again –

THAT SMELL!

Max left the laundry room door and trotted down the steps of the porch, following the scent. His nose in the air, Max stood sniffing the wind, trying to decide which way he should go. Then he caught it – **The Scent.** It was so strong and coming from the direction of the wire fence, beyond the tall grass and forest of trees.

Placing his nose to the ground, Max began to follow the scent. Under the wire fence,

through the tall grass, and into the forest of trees he went. Not realizing he was wandering

farther and farther from home, Max continued to follow the scent, through fields, around

trees, and down a path. At the end of the path, Max stopped and realized he was very tired

and thirsty. The sun had risen some time ago and was now high in the sky.

He continued to follow the scent until he came to a big grassy pasture filled with huge

black animals, with skinny legs, large heads, and big ears. Oh my goodness! Max

took off barking and running at the strange animals. WOOF WOOF WOOF!

Max hopped around from one animal to another, sniffing and barking. He was so excited! He'd never seen such crazy looking creatures in all his life! The odd animals just looked at him with their big black eyes and continued to eat the grass, ignoring Max and his craziness.

Then, he found the scent that made him feel so tingly inside, and he just had to roll in it. He flopped on the ground and rolled from side to side, enjoying this new smell so much. Oh, golly! This was the best day ever!

Once he was content that he had absorbed as much of the smell as he could, he got up, gave himself a good shake, and continued to wander along his way. It wasn't long until Max heard another new sound. CLUCK, CLUCK CLUCK. CLUCK CLUCK CLUCK. BROCK BOCK BOCK. The sound was everywhere! *What was it?*' he wondered.

Running up over the hill, he saw tons of small clucking animals. They were very strange looking, with their weird layered, fluffy fur. It didn't look like any fur Max had ever seen. They had fat bodies with super skinny legs and feet, and their faces had funny pointed noses and tiny round eyes that didn't seem to have any color. On top of their heads were these crazy red spiky things. Max just couldn't help himself. He had to chase these strange animals! So off he leapt barking and chasing and chasing and barking. The clucking animals scattered everywhere, frightened of Max.

Max was so excited, he wanted to wrestle with one. He jumped on top of the one closest to him and started to roll with it, when suddenly he felt something dig deep into his neck. The largest of the Crazy Eyes had grabbed onto Max's neck with its long sharp claws and wouldn't let go! It was flapping around, clucking and pinching Max, forcing him to run away. Once it let go, Max ran away as fast as he could. He didn't want to play with them anymore!

After his battle with the Crazy Eyes, Max was tired and needed a nap. He saw a nice shady area with lots of trees, found a soft cozy spot, and soon fell into a deep sleep.

When Max awoke, he was so thirsty. He had been traveling for hours. He had seen some water near the Crazy Eyes, but he definitely wasn't going back there again! Max placed his nose to the ground and sniffed, hoping to find water.

As he wandered down a path, surrounded by tall waving grass, he came upon a cricket. Oh joy! Max knew crickets, he had played with them in the park, and sometimes one would get in the apartment. Max pressed his nose down on the cricket, then hopped backwards as it jumped. He pounced at the cricket, pawing at it, careful not to actually touch it. Max loved playing with bugs!

MAKING NEW FRIENDS

As he played, Max heard a familiar sound. He stopped and perked his ears to find where it came from. Max heard the sound of children coming from over a hill. As he came to the top of the hill, he stopped to peek out from behind a tree. There were children – and a mommy! They were playing in the water and laughing. Max went bounding over the hill and ran straight up to the boys, staying at the edge of the water.

"Look, a puppy!" cried one of the boys.

"I see that, Ridge. Hi there Little One. What's your name?" asked the nice lady. Max rushed over to her, jumping up to show his affection. "Well, aren't you a friendly little guy - OH, who needs a bath! What HAVE you been rolling in?!"

"He has a tag," said the other boy. Max immediately ran to love on him as well.

"What does it say, Layton?" asked the nice lady.

"I can't keep him still long enough to read it," he said with a giggle. Holding the smelly, wiggly puppy still was not an easy task, but the nice lady held him while Layton read the tag. It said, "MAX" and had an address from the city.

"Hi, Max! How did you get from the city to our little town?" asked the nice lady.

"Can we keep him?" asked the boys.

"I'm sure he belongs to someone. He's probably visiting one of the neighbors, like you're visiting me. We'll make some calls when we get back to the house," she said. "Let's just enjoy playing with him while we can."

Suddenly the lady called out, "Girls," and two dogs that looked kind of like Max came bouncing through the water. They were both so excited to see Max. They bounced around him, sniffing and poking him with their noses.

Max was thrilled! The only time he had played with other dogs was at the dog park, but they had to stay on their leashes and never really got to play.

Max hopped around, sniffing and poking, while the girls did the same. They seemed as happy to meet Max as he was to meet them. They poked Max then ran into the water, barking for him to follow.

Max stopped. WATER! Yea! He had forgotten how thirsty he was. Max rushed to the edge of the creek to sniff the water. It smelled wonderful! Max lapped up the water, filling his tummy with its goodness.

The new friends barked again, telling Max to come play, but Max just looked at them and backed away from the water. *'Go with them – into the water?! Were they crazy?! Water is for drinking and BATHTIME – YUCK!'* he thought. Max did not like baths. He certainly wasn't going to take one when he could be playing. Max barked back at the girls, telling them to come out of the water.

"I don't think Max likes the water. Boys, let's take the dogs up to the pasture to play while I make some phone calls," said the nice lady. The boys called the dogs, who ran after them to the top of the hill. They ran and played, sniffed and explored until the sun went down.

"Come on everyone, time to go in," called the nice lady.

"What about Max?" asked the boys.

"I haven't found anyone who knows Max ,yet. He'll stay with us until we do."

"Yea," shouted the boys! "

"Now don't get too excited. When we find his owners, Max will go home. I'm

sure they're missing him," she said.

Much to Max's disappointment, once inside the nice lady immediately gave him a bath. To his surprise though, it wasn't as bad as he usually thought it was.

After his bath, the boys got Max a bowl full of food and showed him the water bowl. Once he had his tummy full, Max wandered around the new house. He liked it! He especially liked it when the boys called him up on the sofa to cuddle under the covers. Max felt so comfortable, and he was so tired from his adventurous day, that he fell fast asleep.

When Max woke up, he realized the girls were both cuddled next to him. He reached over and licked each of them. It was so nice having new friends!

Max spent the next few weeks playing and learning about life on a farm, and loving being a dog off a leash. He learned the big black animals with the funny ears and skinny legs were called cows and it is NOT okay to bark at them – or roll in their scent. He also learned the Crazy Eyes are called chickens. The girls seemed to be friends with them, but Max thought it best to keep his distance. He didn't want to go through that experience ever again!

One day while they were out exploring, Max came across that smell again – the same smell that had started him on his exciting adventure. He was so thrilled to smell it again, but what was it? He needed to find it!

Just as he started to follow the scent, he heard the nice lady call,

"Girls! Max!"

As much as he wanted to find where the scent was coming from, he also

wanted to please his new friend, so he ran to the house.

FAMILY

As Max walked into the house, he was shocked to be greeted by his family. Oh my goodness! It was so good to see them. He had been having such a good time, he forgot to go home. His family rushed to him, so excited to see him.

"Thank you for taking such good care of him," said Father. "We hope he hasn't been too much trouble. He can be quite a handful."

"Not at all," said the nice lady. "He's been the perfect houseguest!"

"Really?" questioned Mother, thinking about her purses and shoes Max loved so much.

"Absolutely!" exclaimed the nice lady. "We have loved having him. I'm glad I saw your flyer though. I know how much you must have missed him."

"Yes, we have, but I'm not sure what we're going to do," said Father. "You see, we moved here for my job, but now I'm being sent back to the city, and our new apartment building doesn't allow dogs."

"Oh, I see. That is difficult," stated the nice lady. "Umm, would you excuse me just a moment?" she asked as she walked toward the door.

Max followed the nice lady down the stairs and into the barn. "Dear, Max's family is here, but there's a problem. They're moving back to the city and can't take Max with them. I think we should keep him!" she exclaimed. "He's a very good dog, and we all love him so much! What do you think?"

"I don't know. He is a good dog, but do we really *need* another dog?" he questioned.

"Well, the girls are getting older, and I'll have to retire them before too long. Maybe Max could take their place," she said with a smile.

"If that's what you want to do, it's okay with me," he said as he knelt down to pet Max. "He does seem to be a pretty good dog." Max licked the man's hand and wagged his tail. He liked him!

"Max!" she squealed. "You have a new home!" The nice lady scooped Max up into her arms, swinging him around. "Can I be your new mommy, Max? I'll take very good care of you." Max wagged with excitement.

"Let's go tell the boys," she exclaimed, and they ran back to the house.

They found Max's family inside petting the girls. "May we have Max," the nice lady asked before even catching her breath? "We love him so! He has such a sweetness to him, I think he would be the perfect addition to our family and my business."

"Business," asked Father?

"Yes, I work in a school and take my dogs with me. I think Max would love it," she explained!

"Are you sure," asked Mother? "He can be a lot to handle!"

"We're positive! Max has been so at home with all the animals, and he loves roaming around with the girls," she said. "We would love for him to be part of our family, and you are welcome to come visit him anytime you'd like."

After seeing how much Max loved life at Crystal Rock Ranch and how much the nice lady loved him, Max's family agreed. As they loved Max goodbye, the children cried, sad to leave their pet and friend behind. Max licked each of them, showing how much he loved them.

Standing with his new sisters and his new mom and dad, Max watched as his family drove away without him, but he wasn't sad. He was happy to have a new family. He felt at home here and knew this was where he belonged.

Max felt a new adventure coming on. Maybe he would finally find the source of the scent...

School

About the Author

J. L. Huggs lives in Salado, TX and is a school counselor, in Killeen ISD. Ms. Hugs and Max work together to help the children at Peebles Elementary School be ready to learn. Max is an Emotional Support Animal and lives to love.

About the Illustrator

Adriana Klerner lives in Killeen, TX and is a senior in high school. A talented young lady, she loves spending time with her family and is considering a military career. She will continue to illustrate and perfect her craft as long as she can.